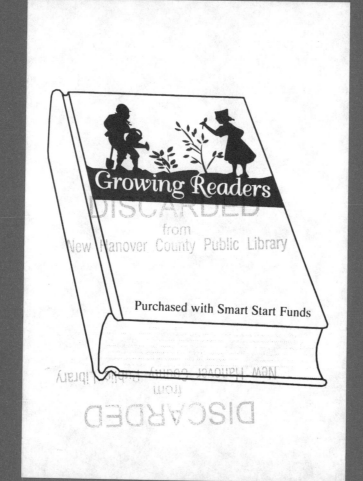

DELIVERY

by **Anastasia Suen**
illustrated by **Wade Zahares**

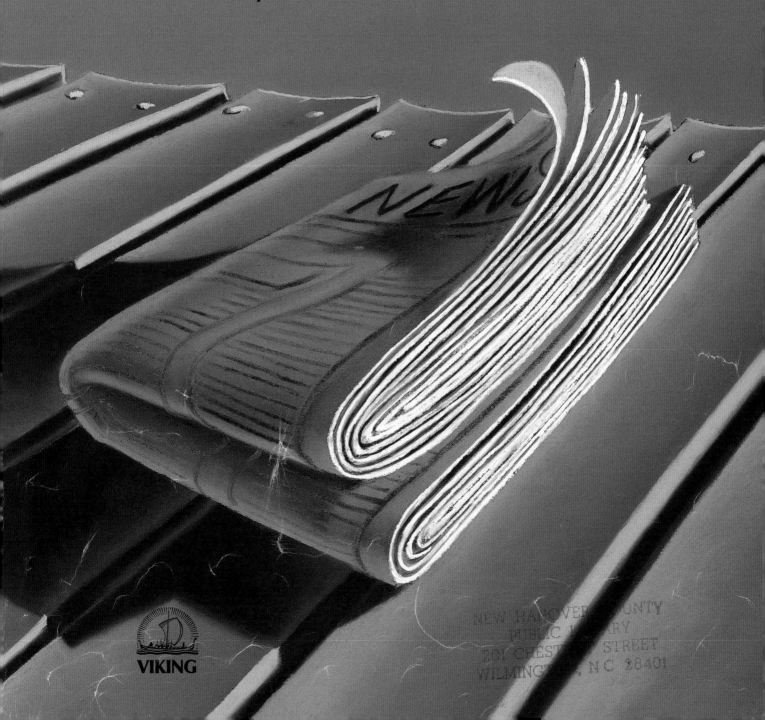

VIKING

VIKING
Published by the Penguin Group
Penguin Putnam Books for Young Readers, 345 Hudson Street,
New York, New York 10014, U.S.A.
Penguin Books Ltd, Registered Offices: Harmondsworth, Middlesex, England

First published in 1999 by Viking,
a division of Penguin Putnam Books for Young Readers.

1 3 5 7 9 10 8 6 4 2

Text copyright © Anastasia Suen, 1999
Illustrations copyright © Wade Zahares, 1999
All rights reserved

LIBRARY OF CONGRESS CATALOGING-IN-PUBLICATION DATA
Suen, Anastasia.
Delivery / by Anastasia Suen ; illustrated by Wade Zahares   p.   cm
Summary: A rhyming look at a number of deliveries that take place in a day,
from a morning newspaper delivery to people being transported by airplanes.
ISBN 0-670-88455-3 (hc)
[1. Delivery of goods Fiction. 2. Stories in rhyme.]
I. Zahares, Wade, ill. II. Title.
PZ8.3.S9354De 1999 [E]–dc21 99-25077 CIP AC

All rights reserved

Printed in Hong Kong
Set in Octogon

For Melanie, editor extraordinaire
—A. S.

For George: Thank you for all your support
in making this book possible.
— W. Z.

Porch views
bring fresh news

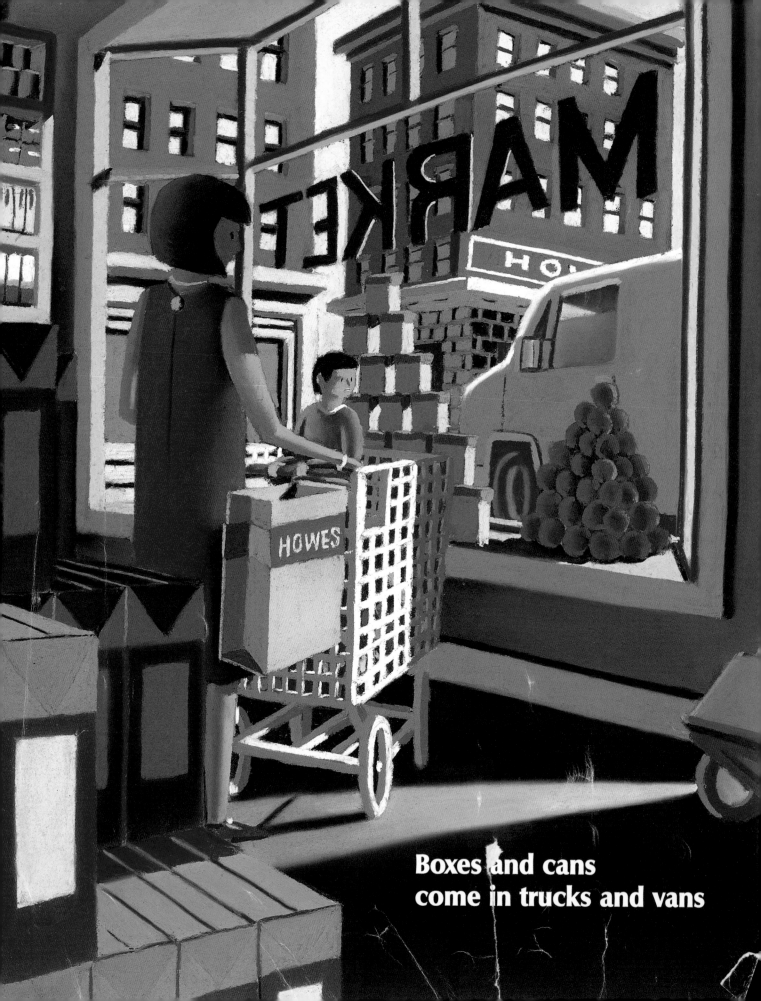

Boxes and cans
come in trucks and vans

**Unwrap it all
for shelves on the wall**

**Flowers flow
to and fro**

**Have you heard
the latest word?**

**Wheels and wings
carry many things**

High and low,
we come and go

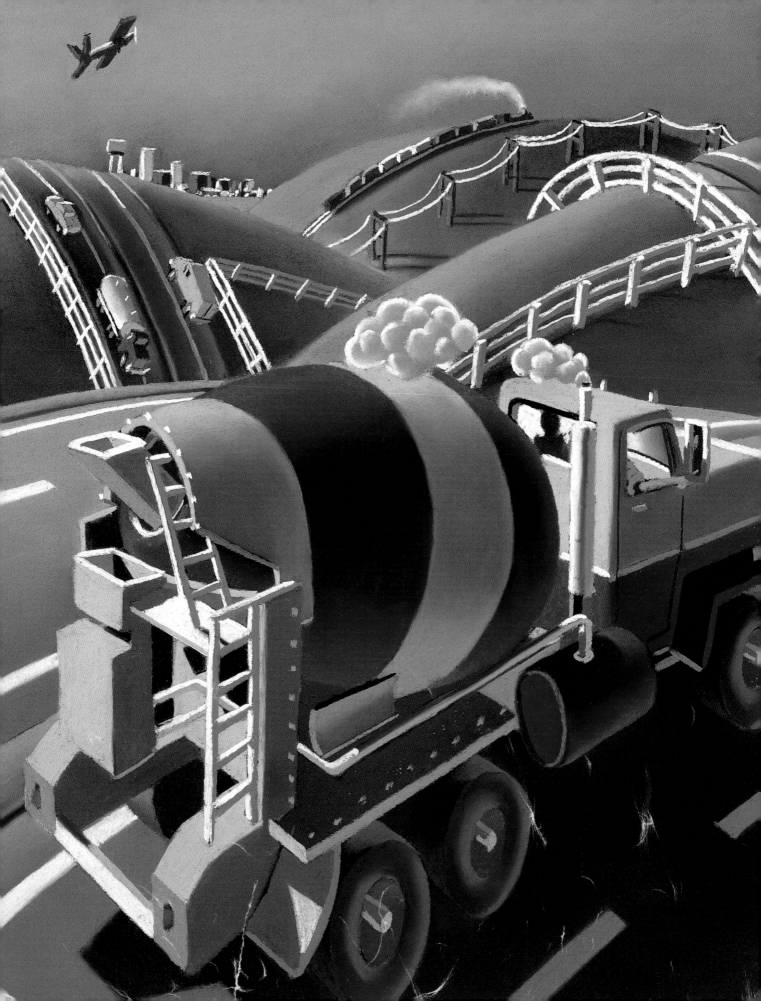

Roll down the road with a heavy load

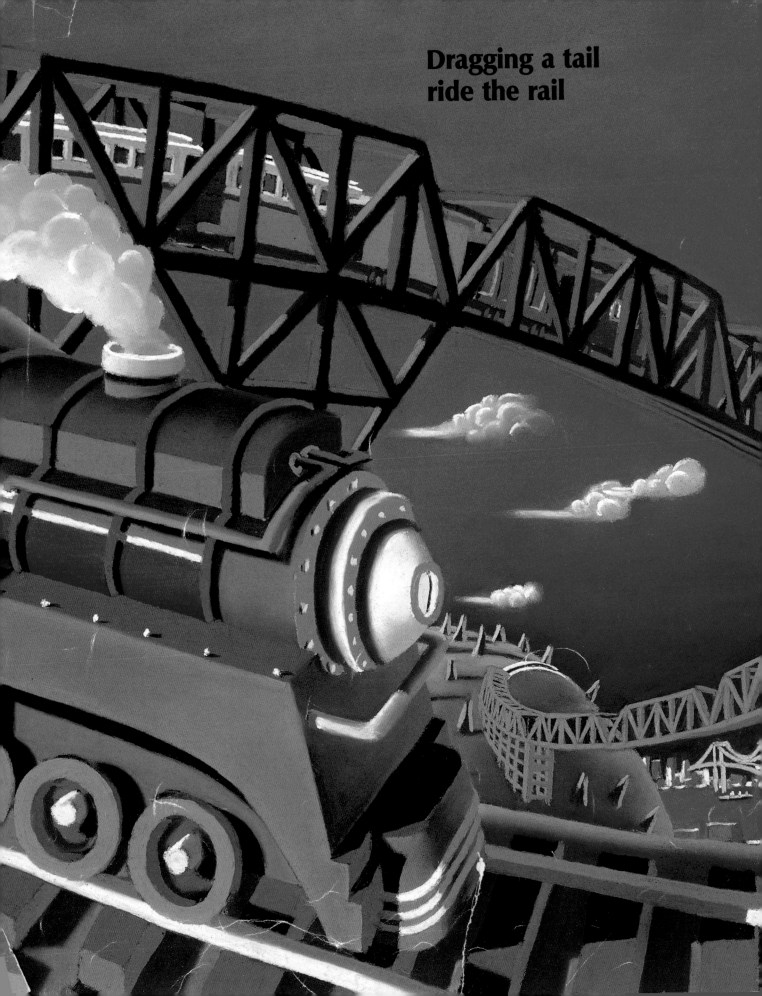

Dragging a tail
ride the rail

**Containers wait
at number eight**

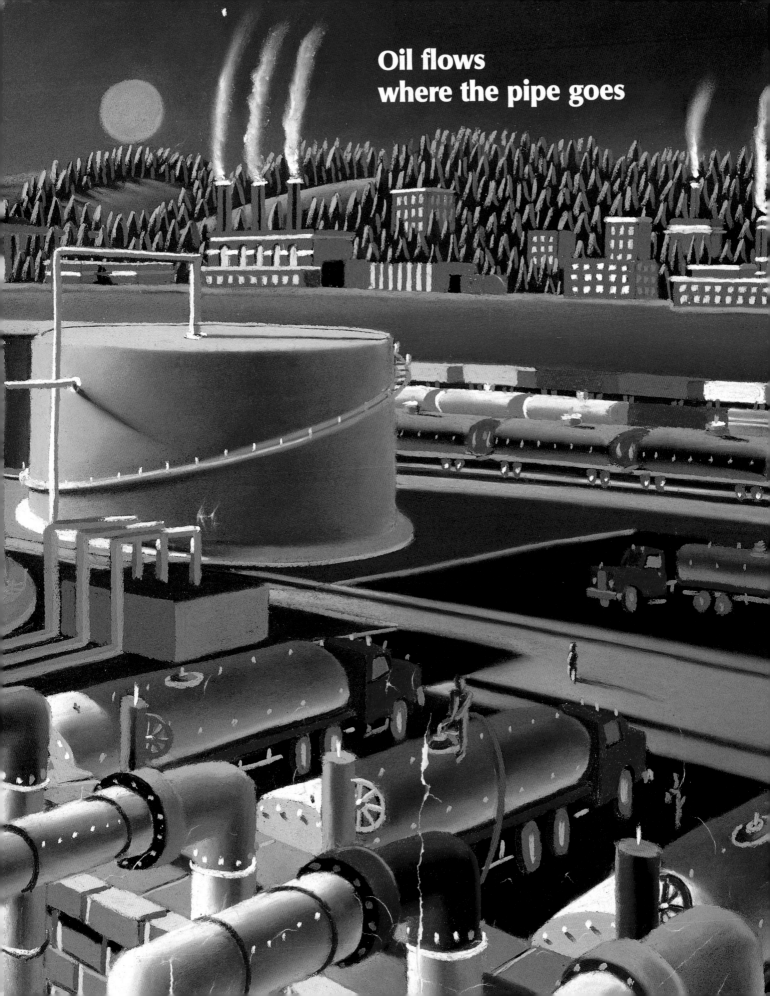

**Oil flows
where the pipe goes**

**From tank to tank
to tank to tank**

On its way,
a new day

Delivery!